My Grandmother's Journey

by *John Cech*

illustrated by Sharon McGinley-Nally

BRADBURY PRESS   NEW YORK

Collier Macmillan Canada   Toronto
Maxwell Macmillan International Publishing Group
New York   Oxford   Singapore   Sydney

10 9 8 7 6 5 4 3 2 1   The text of this book is set in Palatino. Book design by Julie Quan

Library of Congress Cataloging-in-Publication Data, Cech, John. My grandmother's journey / by John Cech ; illustrated by Sharon McGinley-Nally. — 1st ed., 1st American ed.   p.   cm.   Summary: A grandmother tells the story of her eventful life in early twentieth-century Europe and her arrival in the United States after World War II. ISBN 0-02-718135-9. [1. Grandmothers—Fiction.   2. Emigration and immigration—Fiction.]   I. McGinley-Nally, Sharon, ill.   II. Title. PZ7.C29975Hal 1991. [E]—dc20   90-35731 CIP AC

A NOTE FROM THE ARTIST

The illustrations in this book were primarily painted with Rotring Artists Colors (a liquid watercolor that produces very vivid colors), inks, watercolors, acrylics, and occasionally a metallic powdered tempera paint. I use 140 lb. Arches cold press 100% rag watercolor paper, and I usually draw the images first and add color and designs as I proceed. In fact, I'm never really sure what is happening until the painting is done! The finished paintings were color separated using four-color process.

For Feodosia Ivanovna,
who teaches from the heart
of the book of life
—J.C.

For my mother, Helen
—S.M.-N.

I was in bed already when my grandmother came in to say good-night. She pulled off her black shoes and stretched her feet. She held them out and looked at them.

"Feet," she said. "Where haven't you been? What haven't we been through together?"

I liked it when she wiggled her toes and talked to her feet. That's how she got comfortable.

"So, Korie, I think you are waiting for a story."

I nodded.

"What shall it be?"

"Your story, Gramma."

"Ah, now that's a tale full of twists and turns like a path through the woods. I can hardly believe it myself. But my feet could tell you it's true. Let's see. How does it start?"

"When you were a girl."

"Yes, on a cold day in December when I was seven. It was the first time I saw the Gypsies.

The Gypsies came through our village on their way south for the winter in a caravan of wagons drawn by tired horses. I was standing by the gate to our house when I heard the jingling of harness bells. A man, a woman, and their little baby stopped and asked for water, which I ran to get. I begged my mother to let them stay the night with us. The baby cried, and the snowflakes were flying.

"All right," she said. "Just this once."

The young Gypsy woman smiled and let me hold the baby.

"She has a good heart, your daughter," the woman said to my mother. "But I see that she is often ill."

"How did you know that?" My mother was surprised. It was true. I had terrible headaches that nothing and no one could cure.

"Tonight is the first snow. It is a time of healing," the young Gypsy replied. "Let me try to help her."

My mother agreed, wiping tears from her eyes. The doctors in the village had all looked at me and given me medicines. Then they shook their heads, knitted their brows, and grew silent.

After the young woman settled her baby for the night, she took me to a quiet corner of the room. She bathed my temples with the water from the snowflakes that had fallen on the village. She sang to me in her calm, deep voice. The song was old, old. I did not know the words, but they were soft and sure and rocked me quietly with their sound. I glided through the snow clouds and past the moon to a garden, where a river of sweet water ran gently through the grass and angels leaped in the bright blue sky. I leaned over to drink and saw my own face smiling back at me.

Next morning the world was white with new snow. I woke to hear the Gypsy wagon jingling out of town, beyond the orchards. I jumped out of bed and pulled on my boots and ran after it. I have never run so fast, or felt so free and light.

More than ten years passed before another Gypsy stopped at our house. It was spring, and the great meadow that lay on one side of the river was filled with pools of yellow butterflies.

I was a young bride now and came home across the fields and orchards that day to find an old Gypsy woman in the kitchen talking with my mother and some of her friends. She was reading their fortunes on their palms and in the tea leaves.

"Tell me," I said, smiling, "when will I be married?"

"Don't tease me, my girl," the Gypsy replied. "You already are."

She was right. Your grandfather and I had just been married. But no one there had told her.

"And since you are so keen to know your future, I will tell you," she went on. "Today you turn up your nose at dark bread, but there will come a time when you will cry out for even a crust of bread. Today you are strong, but the time will come when you will pray to endure one more hour. You are light on your feet and can dance all night, but there will come a time when your every footstep will be pain."

With that she gathered her shawls around her and left us standing there astonished.

Then, the revolution came, and with it civil war. People who had something suddenly had nothing. We lost our house, our land, our belongings— everything. Every chair, every blanket, right down to the last teacup. The only shelter we could find was the shed where the chickens had lived, so we moved there.

Farmers were yanked from their fields and sent to the army. The Whites and the Reds fought through the countryside, blasting the orchards and burning the wheat. I lost my father and mother and three brothers to the war and hunger that swept the land and to the sickness that followed close behind.

The Gypsy was right. I dreamed about bread—the smell of it baking in the house; tables covered with loaves; slices of bread with butter and jam.

We tried escaping to freedom, but we had no papers to take us over the border, and no money to bribe our way across.

We hid with friends and relatives in different cities until that became too dangerous. Then we traveled into the countryside where we tried to disappear like a tree would or a horse does. We found jobs on farms and in factories, making bricks and harvesting crops—doing whatever we could.

Then came World War II. The enemy marched through our country and took everything—our animals, our crops, our young people. Again we tried to escape to somewhere safe, but soldiers were everywhere, ours and theirs. Both would shoot you if they caught you—they thought you might be a spy.

We hid in a forest while the fighting raged around us. That's where your mother was born, by the banks of a river on a cold March day. When she slept in my arms, I remember thinking that there must still be angels.

We made our way west across the ruined countryside. One night we stopped in a freezing rain outside a lonely farmhouse. We stood shivering, praying it was safe to approach. We knew someone was living there because smoke curled up from the chimney.

In the end, we had to knock on the door. We could not endure the cold another moment. A small thin man opened the door a crack and scowled at us.

"Go away!" he said. "We don't have anything!"

"Please," I pleaded. "We have a child. Perhaps a little milk or a few minutes to get warm again."

The man's face lit up. "A child! In this world!"

He opened the door wide and waved us in. Soon his wife appeared, and their two young daughters climbed through a hidden door from the cellar. They brought up a basket and unpacked it onto the table—cheese and apples, butter and bread!

They passed the baby around and kissed and hugged and marveled over her. They fed us until we couldn't move, and they insisted that we stay with them.

But we knew we needed to press on.

"At least leave the child with us," the woman urged. "She'll be safe here. We'll care for her like our own."

"No," I had to say. "I would always wonder what became of her."

We said good-bye and started walking, dodging the soldiers, sleeping in the woods or wherever we could find a safe place. We carried your mother in our arms. She was the one gift of hope we'd had in all those days.

Whenever anyone saw her, little miracles happened. Somehow, from nothing, there came a little something for her to eat and a little bit more to keep us going. Once, we were trying to find our way through the winding streets of a small city. I was barefoot by now, walking in pain. Out of an alleyway a man suddenly appeared and quickly pressed a pair of shoes into my hands. "They were my wife's," he said. "She would have wanted you to have them." And then he was gone before I could thank him for his kindness.

Your grandfather found what work he could, as a carpenter, a stonemason, a gardener. He was a wizard with his hands. Once, in payment for fixing his roof, a man gave us an old baby buggy and some potatoes. We filled the buggy with your mother and our bundles and pushed it over the mountains. Your grandfather even sang as we went that day. His voice soared up the sides of the hills, and people working in the fields stood up to listen.

We kept carrying our baby and walking west, always to the west, through what was left of our old world. The retreating enemy soldiers captured us and took us and thousands of others back to their country to work in their factories. And that was where we were when peace came. Your mother was a little girl like you when we finally sailed by the Statue of Liberty and stood for the first time in America.

The Gypsy told me many things, Korie. But she did not tell me that the rest of my fortune would be to survive and bring a child out of that place. She did not tell me that I would eat bread again, in a warm house, where I can rest my feet, these old friends, that have carried me halfway around the world to you.

A Note on the Story

  This story is based on events in the life of a remarkable grandmother, Feodosia Ivanovna Belevtsov, who was born in prerevolutionary Russia in 1907; survived the Russian Revolution and the years of the civil war between the Mensheviks (the Whites) and Bolsheviks (the Reds); survived the purges of Stalin and the famines of the 1930s; and, finally, survived capture by the retreating Nazis, who took her, her husband, baby, and tens of thousands of others back to Germany as slave laborers. She came to America after the liberation of Germany at the end of World War II. Her life and its story stand as witness to these events—to their unparalleled destruction and cruelty, to the small miracles that sometimes happened in the midst of such destruction, and to the larger miracle—that such things are endured and rare lights like hers emerge to shed their radiance on the darkness.

E
C
      Cech, John
      My Grandmother's ᴊᴏᴜᴿᴺᴇʏX
      Journey

16058

E		
C		
AUTHOR		
Cech, John		
TITLE		
My Grandmother's Journey		
DATE DUE	BORROWER'S NAME	ROOM NUMBER
	JDL	129
4/17	Alissa T.	421 N
10/6	Sarah KB